ALONG CAME TOM

For Tom

A Red Fox Book

Published by Random Century Children's Books
20 Vauxhall Bridge Road, London SW1V 2SA

A division of the Random Century Group
London Melbourne Sydney Auckland
Johannesburg and agencies throughout the world

First published by The Bodley Head Children's Books 1990

Copyright © John Prater 1990

Red Fox edition 1992

The right of John Prater to be identified as the author and
illustrator of this work has been asserted by him in accordance
with the Copyright, Designs and Patents Act, 1988.

Printed in Hong Kong

ISBN 0 09 992150 2

JOHN PRATER

ALONG CAME TOM

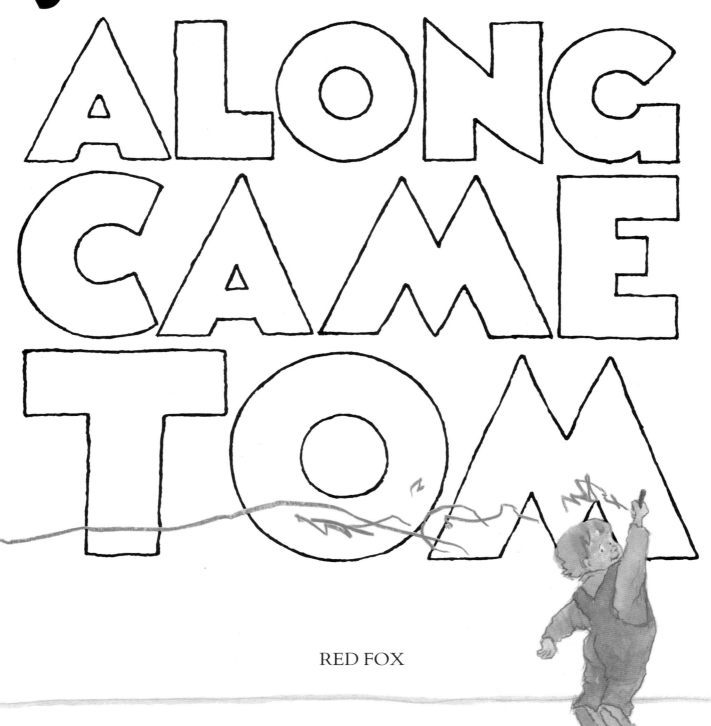

RED FOX

All was quiet in the house,

until Tom woke up.

We had breakfast together.

After breakfast we played at dressing-up

. . . but then along came Tom.

Mum wanted to take our photo

. . . but along came Tom.

Click!

It was a lovely day so we played
in the garden.

Then we built a den

. . . but along came Tom.

After lunch we did some drawing

. . . and so did Tom.

Then we gave the toys a party.

We got out a very difficult jigsaw.

We'd nearly finished it

. . . when along came Tom.

So we tried to watch TV

. . . with Tom.

After tea we helped to clear up.

Tom wasn't much help though.

Then came the best part of the whole day.

"Come along Tom, it's time for bed."

"Goodnight Tom."

Some bestselling Red Fox picture books

THE BIG ALFIE AND ANNIE ROSE STORYBOOK
by Shirley Hughes
OLD BEAR
by Jane Hissey
JOHN PATRICK NORMAN McHENNESSY –
THE BOY WHO WAS ALWAYS LATE
by John Burningham
I WANT A CAT
by Tony Ross
NOT NOW, BERNARD
by David McKee
THE STORY OF HORRIBLE HILDA AND HENRY
by Emma Chichester Clark
THE SAND HORSE
by Michael Foreman and Ann Turnbull
BAD BORIS GOES TO SCHOOL
by Susie Jenkin-Pearce
MRS PEPPERPOT AND THE BILBERRIES
by Alf Prøysen
BAD MOOD BEAR
by John Richardson
WHEN SHEEP CANNOT SLEEP
by Satoshi Kitamura
THE LAST DODO
by Ann and Reg Cartwright
IF AT FIRST YOU DO NOT SEE
by Ruth Brown
THE MONSTER BED
by Jeanne Willis and Susan Varley
DR XARGLE'S BOOK OF EARTHLETS
by Jeanne Willis and Tony Ross
JAKE
by Deborah King